KNIGHTMARE

For Lucy, Theo and Tara
(Team Bently Curtin) – PB

For Clarey, Bonnie and Sonny
(Team Blunt) – FB

STRIPES PUBLISHING
An imprint of Little Tiger Press
1 The Coda Centre, 189 Munster Road,
London SW6 6AW

A paperback original
First published in Great Britain in 2014

Text copyright © Peter Bently, 2014
Illustrations copyright © Fred Blunt, 2014

ISBN: 978-1-84715-433-0

The right of Peter Bently and Fred Blunt to be identified as the
author and illustrator of this work respectively has been asserted
by them in accordance with the Copyright, Designs and Patents
Act, 1988.

Printed and bound in the UK.

10 9 8 7 6 5 4 3 2 1

KNIGHTMARE

Life Stinks!

PETER BENTLY

Illustrated by Fred Blunt

Stripes

TEAM PERCY

CASTLE BOMBAST

Sir Percy the Proud

Cedric
Thatchbottom
(Me!)

Patchcoat the Jester

Margaret the Cook

TEAM ROLAND

BLACKSTONE FORT

Sir Roland the Rotten

Walter Warthog

Guards of Blackstone Fort

Chapter One

A Scroll for Breakfast

"Cedric!"

"Yes, Sir Percy?"

"Have you groomed Prancelot?"

"Yes, Sir Percy."

"And polished my armour?"

"Yes, Sir Percy."

"And fluffed up my plumes?"

"Yes, Sir Percy."

"Splendid. Now where's my breakfast?"

"Coming, Sir Percy!"

I entered the bedchamber and placed the breakfast tray on the bedside table. Then I went over to the window and pulled back the thick embroidered curtains.

Sir Percy Piers Peregrine de Bluster de Bombast opened an eye and blinked in the bright sunlight.

"So, what's Margaret made for me this morning?" he said cheerfully.

He sat up in bed and I placed the tray on his lap. "Porridge, Sir Percy."

His face fell at the sight of the lumpy, greenish gloop.

KNIGHTMARE

"*Again?*"

"Yes, Sir Percy."

"Thank you, Cedric," he groaned. "That will be all for now. Come back in half an hour and help me dress. Today I'm going for a ride in my new armour – to give it a bit of an airing before the tournament."

"Yes, Sir Percy."

I headed back down to the kitchen for my own breakfast dose of Mouldybun Margaret's porridge.

Yeucchh! I can't blame Sir Percy for being disappointed. It looks EXACTLY like the stuff they were carting away when Sir Percy had the castle moat cleaned last week. Smells like it, too.

KNIGHTMARE

Maybe I'd better start at the very beginning. My name is Cedric Thatchbottom and I've been working at Castle Bombast for a month now. I'm Sir Percy's squire, which means one day I'll be a KNIGHT like him and I'll get to do to cool stuff like:

1. Wear ARMOUR

2. Have a SWORD

3. Rescue DAMSELS IN DISTRESS
(Whatever *damsels* are. Some kind of pet?)

HELP

4. Defeat an entire army of BADDIES single-handedly and save the kingdom

5. Boss around PEOPLE WHO LAUGH AT MY NAME (and my red hair)

KNIGHTMARE

I've wanted to be a knight for as long as I can remember. But you can't be a knight without being a squire first. One day I was out helping my dad (Ethelred Thatchbottom, builder to the gentry) when I spotted a sheet of parchment pinned to a tree:

SQUIRE REQUIRED
to serve celebrated local knight.
No experience necessary.
Apply to Sir Percy P.P. de Bluster de Bombast, Castle Bombast.

I nagged my mum and dad to let me try out for the job.

"Don't be silly," said Dad. "Only toffs get to be squires and we ain't toffs, Ced."

KNIGHTMARE

I nagged them some more and eventually they said there was no harm in trying but I shouldn't get my hopes up.

So I went to see Sir Percy, and to my amazement I got the job! Soon after that I came to live at Castle Bombast to look after Sir Percy and do all his chores.

Sir Percy is always promising to teach me proper knight stuff, but he never seems to get round to it. Maybe he's just too busy being a celebrity. People call him Sir Percy the Proud and he's famous for being the bravest, kindest, cleverest and most handsome knight in the kingdom. It says so in *The Song of Percy*. Sir Percy wrote *The Song of Percy*, so I guess he should know.

KNIGHTMARE

As I entered the kitchen, Mouldybun Margaret came bustling past me with a large steaming platter.

"Clear some space on that bench," she barked. "'Urry up, Carrot-top! These apple and pig's liver cookies is 'ot!"

I shoved a few things out of the way and Margaret plonked down the platter.

"That's better," she said. She nodded at a battered old pot over the kitchen fire. "You can 'elp yerself to porridge. And keep yer thievin' 'ands off my cookies. They're for Sir Percy."

"Yikes! His poor tummy!" muttered

KNIGHTMARE

Patchcoat the Jester, who was sitting at
the long kitchen table.

"What's that?" snapped Margaret.

"Oh, nothing," said Patchcoat innocently.
"I just said those cookies look yummy!"

Margaret snorted and stomped off. I
plopped a ladleful of porridge into a wooden
bowl and sat next to Patchcoat. He's been
my best friend since I came to work here.

KNIGHTMARE

"Here, Ced, I've got another new joke," Patchcoat said. "*Knock! Knock!*"

"Who's there?" I mumbled, coming across something hard in my porridge. *Ugh!* I spat out a lump of gristly bone.

"Armour," said Patchcoat.

"Armour who?" I sighed.

"Armour getting outta here!" cried Patchcoat. He leaped out of his chair and ran from the kitchen, giggling. "I'm off to work. See ya later, Ced— OOF!"

Patchcoat had bumped right into Walter Warthog, who had come into the castle without knocking.

"Mind where you're going, you oaf!" said Walter, pushing Patchcoat out of the way and marching into the kitchen.

Walter is the squire of Sir Roland the Rotten, who is famous for being the nastiest knight in the kingdom. I'd met Sir Roland for the first time just a couple of days earlier, when Sir Percy was out hunting with his best mate, Sir Spencer the Splendid. (Guess who got to carry all the bows and arrows. And lunch.) This huge wild boar ran past us and Sir Percy cracked a joke that went something like, "What's fat and bristly and grunts like a pig? Sir Roland the Rotten!" Then who should ride out of the bushes after the boar but Sir Roland himself! He gave Sir Percy a right rotten stare and galloped off without a word.

KNIGHTMARE

I tried not to laugh as Patchcoat stuck his tongue out at Walter behind his back.

Walter looked at me and sneered. "Morning, Squire Squirt!" he said. "Lazing about instead of working, I see. You'll never be a knight at this rate!"

(I HATE it when Walter calls me Squire Squirt. Just because I'm two years younger than him and my family aren't posh.)

"What do you want, Wartface?" I said.

Walter thrust something under my nose. It was a scroll of parchment, rolled up tightly and sealed with a blob of red wax. The wax was stamped with a boar's head and two crossed battleaxes – the badge of Sir Roland the Rotten.

"Letter for Sir Percy the Pompous," he said. "Whoops! I mean Percy the *Proud*."

I glared at him.

"Why would Sir Roland be writing to Sir Percy?" I asked. "Is it something to do with the tournament?"

"You'll find out soon enough," grinned

KNIGHTMARE

Walter unpleasantly. "See you Thursday at the tournament, Fatbottom. That is, if they allow ginger peasants into the royal palace!"

"Hey!" I said.

But Walter had already marched out of the kitchen, sneaking one of Mouldybun Margaret's cookies when she wasn't looking.

Wait till he tastes it, I thought. *That'll serve him right for being rude!*

I took the scroll up to Sir Percy. He was still in bed, picking at his half-eaten bowl of porridge.

"Letter for you, Sir Percy," I said, holding out the scroll.

KNIGHTMARE

Sir Percy shot upright in bed and snatched it from my hand.

"A fan letter!" he beamed. "They'll be asking for a signed copy of *The Song of Percy.* You must send them one at once. Dear me, at this rate I shall soon run out!"

"It's not a fan letter, Sir Percy—"

"Ah," said Sir Percy. A dreamy smile spread over his face. "Of course. It'll be from a fair lady. Yet another proposal of marriage. Cedric, it's a hard life being such a famous, brave and handsome knight! You shall have to write and turn her down, just like all the others! Unless – um – she happens to be a rich princess, in which case I suppose I *might* – um – consider—"

KNIGHTMARE

"It's from Sir Roland," I said.

Sir Percy's dreamy smile vanished.

"F-from Sir Roland?" he said. "Why would he be writing to me?"

"No idea, Sir Percy," I said. "I *think* it might be about the tournament."

He unrolled the scroll and read it.

"Blithering battleaxes!" Sir Percy flopped back on to his pillows, dropping the scroll. He seemed to have gone a bit pale.

"Are you feeling all right, Sir Percy?"

I picked up the scroll and read it.

"Sir Roland's challenged you to a joust!" I gasped.

24

Deer Sir Persy,

So I'm just like a wild boar, am I? You are going to be ~~inkerdibley~~ ~~incrediatly~~ so sorry you insulted me! I challinge you to a JOUST at the king's Tournament on Thursday. And guess wot? I'm going to win! So there.

Yours Rottenly,

Sir Roland Ronald Roger de Basham-Flatt

Chapter Two

Sir Percy's Underpants

I read the letter again. Sir Roland the Rotten had challenged Sir Percy to a joust. And not just any old joust.

"This is amazing, Sir Percy!" I said. "Sir Roland wants to joust with you at the tournament! Imagine his face when you knock him off his horse in front of all the other knights!"

KNIGHTMARE

Sir Percy sank deeper into his pillows. "All the other knights…" he muttered. He really was looking very pale.

"*And* in front of the king and queen!" I said.

"Ohhh!" Sir Percy let out a little wail and pulled his covers up over his head.

I don't blame him. The excitement was almost too much for me, too.

"Do you want me to write back to Sir Roland straight away, Sir Percy?" I said to the lump in the bedclothes. "I'll tell him what it says in *The Song of Percy.* The bit that goes *Sir Percy fears no mortal knight. He's never lost a single fight!* I can't wait to see you in action!"

27

KNIGHTMARE

"Stop!" Sir Percy sat up again. "My dear Cedric, I'd simply *love* to fight Sir Roland. But I've just realized I can't!"

"Oh," I said, disappointed. "But why not, Sir Percy?"

"It's out of the question, dear boy," said Sir Percy. "I can't fight anyone with my bad leg, you know... *Ooh!* There it goes again!"

KNIGHTMARE

"Bad leg?" I said. "I didn't know you had a bad leg, Sir Percy."

Sir Percy winced. "Oh, didn't I mention it?" he said. "Old battle injury, you know. You must have noticed my limp. Left leg flares up from time to time – *ouch!* – the pain! I can't possibly fight Sir Roland in this condition. You'll have to write him a note excusing me from the tournament."

Then I remembered something I'd read in *The Song of Percy.*

"Sir Percy," I cried. "Your pants!"

"There's no need to be rude, dear boy," said Sir Percy.

"No, I mean your *magic* pants," I gabbled. "The pair that wizard gave you

KNIGHTMARE

in *The Song of Percy*, remember? What was the spell again? *However injured you may be, these pants will bring you victory!*"

Sir Percy sat there opening and closing his mouth like a fish. "Ah … yes," he said eventually. "*Those* magic pants."

"I'll fetch them," I said. "They probably need an iron before Friday."

I dashed over to Sir Percy's wardrobe, but Sir Percy called me back.

"Wait, Cedric!" He smiled breezily. "Um – first go and fetch me a quill, ink and a sheet of parchment. I shall write to Sir Roland myself. Not only will I accept his silly challenge, I'll also show him how much better my spelling is!"

KNIGHTMARE

"Very good, Sir Percy," I said.

I hurried downstairs to Sir Percy's study and grabbed his writing things. When I got back, he was standing in the enormous fireplace with his head up the chimney.

"Sir Percy?" I said.

For someone with a dodgy leg Sir Percy jumped out of the fireplace amazingly quickly.

KNIGHTMARE

"Oh! There you are, Cedric," said Sir Percy hastily. "I was just – um – checking to see if the chimney was blocked. Bit smoky in here, don't you think?"

It didn't seem smoky at all to me. But I said, "Maybe I'd better let in a bit of fresh air, Sir Percy." I opened a window, only to hear Patchcoat down below, trying out a new joke on Grunge the gardener.

"*Knock! Knock!*" said Patchcoat.

"Oo be there?" Grunge grunted.

"Cows go!" said Patchcoat.

"Cows go 'oo?" said Grunge.

"No, they don't, cows go *moo*!" cackled Patchcoat. "Get it?"

"No," said Grunge.

KNIGHTMARE

I turned to Sir Percy, who had limped back into bed. (Despite what Sir Percy said, I'd *never* noticed his limp before.)

"Ah, splendid, you brought the quill and parchment," he said, plumping up his pillows. "Now, I'll write to Sir Roland while you go and give my – um – magic underpants an iron. It's the yellow spotty pair."

"Yes, Sir Percy!" I beamed. This was more like it. Sir Percy seemed to be back to his normal self. I went to the wardrobe and opened the drawer where Sir Percy kept all his underpants.

It was empty!

"Something the matter, Cedric?" said Sir Percy.

33

"Your underpants!" I gasped. "They're not here!"

"Really?" said Sir Percy. "Good gracious, I wonder how on *earth* that can have happened."

"Perhaps they've been stolen, Sir Percy!" I spluttered.

"Stolen, eh?" Sir Percy shook his head slowly and tutted. "I daresay you're right, dear boy. Well, well, well. Stolen. Oh dear."

"You must organize a search!" I said. "You must catch the thief!"

"A search?" Sir Percy smiled. "Oh no, my dear Cedric. The thief is probably miles away by now!" He sighed. "Well, with this leg of mine – *ouch!* – a joust is absolutely

34

out of the question if I don't have my magic
pants. How sad. You'd better write that note
to Sir Roland after all."

Then I remembered something else. The
most important thing of all.

"But Sir Percy!" I said. "You *have* to fight
Sir Roland."

"*Have* to, Cedric?" guffawed Sir Percy.
"You are forgetting that I am a knight!
A knight doesn't *have* to do *anything*, my
dear boy."

"But it's in the Knight's Code of Honour,
Sir Percy," I reminded him. "A knight who
refuses a challenge shall suffer *eternal
shame and dishonour.*"

Sir Percy stopped laughing. He seemed

to have gone rather pale again.

"Are you all right, Sir Percy?" I asked.

"Yes, I'm – er – fine, dear boy," he shivered. "Just a tad – um – chilly."

"No problem," I said. "I'll put another log on the fire."

I stepped over to the fireplace, but Sir Percy suddenly leaped out of bed.

"No, no!" he said, grabbing my arm. "There's no need! Honestly, I'm quite warm enough!"

But I wasn't really listening. I had just noticed something. A little way up the chimney there's a ledge where I put Sir Percy's late-night mug of spiced milk and honey to keep warm. Something had

KNIGHTMARE

been stuffed into a corner of the ledge.
I gave it a tug and into the fireplace
tumbled a great heap of – underpants!

"Look!" I gasped, pulling a yellow and
spotty pair out of the heap and shaking off
a bit of soot. "It's your magic pants!
I wonder how they got up the chimney?"

"Yes," said Sir Percy. "I wonder."

"Maybe the thief was disturbed and hid them there before he escaped," I suggested.

"Yes, yes … maybe," groaned Sir Percy.

"Sir Percy, this is brilliant!" I said. "Now you've got your magic underpants back, Sir Roland doesn't stand a chance! It's going to be such an amazing joust. I can't wait till Thursday!"

But I don't think Sir Percy heard me. He seemed to have fainted.

I know this sounds ridiculous, but it was almost as if he didn't want to fight Sir Roland. If I didn't know any better I'd almost say he was… But no, that's impossible. The hero of *The Song of Percy* could never, ever be *scared*. Could he?

Chapter Three

What the
Apothecary Ordered

It didn't take long for news of the joust to spread. Walter must have boasted about it to everyone he met on the way back to Blackstone Fort. I know this because at lunchtime on Tuesday a troupe of travelling players in a big covered wagon called at the castle.

"Good day, young master!" said the

troupe leader, with an elaborate bow. "Perkin's the name, entertainment's the game! Can I interest you in our play?"

"Sure!" I said. "What are you doing? *Saint George and the Dragon?*"

"Nah," said Perkin. "We're working on a brand-new play. We met a chap on the road who told us about a joust between his master and some useless knight called Sir Percy. Here, take a look."

He handed me a piece of parchment.

Coming Soon!

MASTER PERKIN'S PLAYERS PRESENT

Strictly Come Lancing
OR
The Piercing of Sir Percy

GUTS 'N' GORE GUARANTEED!
ALL ENQUIRIES AT
THE BOAR'S BOTTOM INN

"Right," I frowned. "I'm not interested, thanks."

"Ah well, suit yourself," said Perkin. "We're staying at the Boar's Bottom if you change your mind."

"I won't," I said. "But thanks, anyway."

41

KNIGHTMARE

By teatime I was starting to get really worried. Sir Percy was still refusing to get out of bed, complaining about his old leg wound, and we were supposed to be leaving for the palace the next day. So far, all I'd packed were his lucky underpants. But which suit of armour was he going to wear? How many helmets should I pack? Would he prefer the red plume or the yellow one?

"Maybe he's really sick," I said to Patchcoat in the kitchen.

"Well, there's one way to find out," said Patchcoat. "What we need is an apothecary."

"A pot of what?" I said.

"An apothecary," he grinned. "You know, someone who heals people. Where did you say those actors were staying?"

"The Boar's Bottom," I said. "Why? I told them we weren't interested."

"I've just had an idea," chuckled Patchcoat. "I won't be long. See you in a bit!"

Half an hour later there was a knock on the kitchen door. I opened it to see an old man in a long black robe carrying a large leather bag and a staff. His face was almost completely hidden beneath a white beard and a floppy black cap. A pair of newfangled

43

eye-glasses perched on the end of his nose.
They made his eyes look like pickled onions
floating in a jar of vinegar.

"Can I help you?" I asked. "I told the
guards not to let in any cold-callers."

"Good day to you!" wheezed the man.
"Doctor Bartholomew Leechwell at your
service. Travelling apothecary to the gentry.

Gashes, mashes and
bashes a speciality.
Somebody by the name
of Patchcoat sent me
here. I gather your
master is unwell?"

"Oh right," I said.
"You'd better come in."

KNIGHTMARE

I led Dr Leechwell upstairs to Sir Percy's chamber and knocked on the door. There was an odd scurrying noise and then Sir Percy's feeble voice said, "Enter!"

I went into the room and bowed.

Sir Percy was lying in bed. "What is it, Cedric?" he quavered.

"How's your leg, Sir Percy?" I asked.

"Oooh, the agony!" he groaned. "There's really no way I can take part in the tournament."

"I've brought someone to see you," I said. "Come in, Dr Leechwell."

The apothecary entered. "Good afternoon, Sir Percy," he said. "Problem with your leg, eh?"

"Er – well – yes," mumbled Sir Percy. "But it's only an old battle wound, you know. There's really no need to bother—"

"Ah! Such admirable courage," interrupted Dr Leechwell cheerfully. "Just like a true knight! I have tended to the wounds of many knights and nobles. My cures are renowned all over the kingdom!"

"You mean all your patients have recovered?" I asked.

Dr Leechwell paused and scratched his beard. "Well, let's just say that one way or another my patients are – ahem – no longer in pain," he chuckled. "Now, let's take a look at this leg." He whipped off the bedclothes.

KNIGHTMARE

"Aargh!" squealed Sir Percy, quickly pulling down his nightshirt over his knobbly knees.

"Oh, don't mind me, old chap!" cackled Dr Leechwell. "Seen it all before! So, which is the leg with the wound?"

"Er – the right one," said Sir Percy.

(Funny, I was sure he'd said the *left* one before.)

Dr Leechwell peered at Sir Percy's right leg. He tutted and slowly shook his head. "Dear me," he said. "This is worse than I thought. *Much* worse." He called me over to look. "What do you see there, lad?"

"Well – nothing, actually," I answered truthfully.

"Precisely!" said Dr Leechwell. "The wound is invisible to the naked eye. The very worst type. It can mean only one thing. An evil spirit has entered Sir Percy's leg. Nasty."

"*What?*" said Sir Percy, sitting up. "But that's imposs—" He suddenly glanced at me. "Um – I mean, er – are you *sure*, doctor?"

"No doubt about it!" said Dr Leechwell. "But not to worry, Sir Percy. I have the very cure!"

He rummaged in his bag and pulled out a small pottery jar. He opened the jar. Inside was a wriggling mass of slimy black things.

"Yeuch!" I said. "What are *those*?"

KNIGHTMARE

"Bloodsucking leeches," smiled the apothecary. "They will suck the evil spirit from the wound. Apply two leeches three times a day, as required."

"Nooo!" yelped Sir Percy. "Take them away!"

"But these are the very finest leeches," said the doctor.

"I don't care!" said Sir Percy. "I hate creepy-crawlies!"

(Which seemed a bit odd, considering he'd seen off a giant spider in *The Song of Percy*...)

49

KNIGHTMARE

"Very well," said the apothecary. "I shall have to try another method."

This time he fished a knife and a brass bowl out of his bag. He spat on the blade and rubbed it on his sleeve.

"Er – I say – *what* exactly are you going to do with that thing?" asked Sir Percy, shrinking back into his pillows.

"Oh, just open a vein or two in your leg, Sir Percy," smiled Dr Leechwell. "A little bloodletting works wonders, you know. Master Cedric, if you would kindly hold the bowl to catch the blood."

"No way!" wailed Sir Percy. "I can't bear the sight of blood. Especially my own!"

(Which also seemed a bit strange for

someone who had been in all those battles in *The Song of Percy*.)

"In that case, Sir Percy," sighed Dr Leechwell. "There is only one other way to sort out your leg." He rummaged in his bag and produced a small length of wood. "Now then. When I say 'ready', I want you to pop this in your mouth and bite down hard."

"Ready?" said Sir Percy. "Ready for what?"

Dr Leechwell reached into his bag yet again. This time he pulled out a rusty saw. "Ready to cut off that nasty leg of yours!" he said brightly. "We'll have you back on your feet in no time. Or should I say back

51

on your *foot*. Ha! Just my little joke!"

"Aargh!" Sir Percy leaped out of bed and cowered behind me. "Cedric, get that man away from me!" he squawked. "He's not coming anywhere near me with that saw!"

KNIGHTMARE

"Ah. Then perhaps you would prefer me to use your own sword, Sir Percy?" smiled Dr Leechwell. "One swift strike should do the trick."

Sir Percy pushed me forward. "C-Cedric, kindly show Dr Leechwell out," he said. "My leg has made a miraculous recovery!"

"Are you *sure?*" said Dr Leechwell.

"*Quite* sure," said Sir Percy.

"Can't I cut off just a *little* bit?" asked the doctor.

"No!" squealed Sir Percy. "Go away!"

"Very well, Sir Percy," sighed Dr Leechwell. "But let me know if it flares up again. Good day!"

The apothecary bowed politely. I held

the door open as he walked out of the room. As he passed me I could have sworn he *winked.* Weird.

But not as weird as what happened next. As soon as he was out of sight of Sir Percy, Dr Leechwell took off his eye-glasses – and his beard!

"Patchcoat!" I gasped.

"Phew, that's better," he said. "Those eye-glass things were pinching my nose. And I was sweating like a pig under all that fuzz!"

"But what – how…?" I spluttered.

"Shh!" Patchcoat grinned. "Keep your voice down, Ced! Now I've fixed Sir Percy I'd better head off to the Boar's Bottom. I need to give Master Perkin his apothecary costume back!"

He scuttled off down the corridor and I hurried back to Sir Percy.

"I'm so pleased your leg is better, Sir Percy," I said. "Now you'll be able to go ahead with the joust. Shall I start to pack for the trip?"

Sir Percy whimpered.

"It's just as well, Sir Percy," I said. "I know it sounds silly, but if you'd said you were injured Sir Roland *might* have thought you were trying to get out of the fight. Er – not that you are, of course. But he might smell a rat."

Sir Percy stopped whimpering. "What did you say, dear boy?"

"Not that you are," I repeated.

"No, the next bit."

"He might smell a rat, Sir Percy," I said.

"Mmm, I wonder…" said Sir Percy. He suddenly bounded out of bed. "Cedric, come with me to the armoury. We must prepare for the tournament!"

Chapter Four

The Road
to the Palace

I spent the rest of the day and the next morning packing Sir Percy's clothes. He took so long choosing the plume to wear in his helmet that I had to remind him to pack a few weapons, too.

Once I'd finished loading up the mule cart that was carrying all our trunks, I helped Sir Percy into his armour.

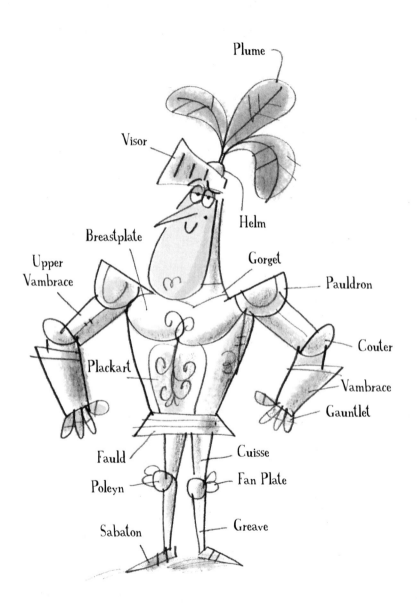

Plume

Visor

Helm

Breastplate

Gorget

Upper
Vambrace

Pauldron

Couter

Plackart

Vambrace

Gauntlet

Fauld

Cuisse

Poleyn

Fan Plate

Sabaton

Greave

KNIGHTMARE

It's no easy matter strapping about thirty pieces of iron on to a master who's a bit of a fidget *and* ticklish into the bargain. But at last we were ready to leave for the royal castle of Goldentowers.

As Sir Percy mounted his horse, Prancelot, I felt a great surge of pride. No knight could have looked more dashing than he did up there in the saddle. His armour gleamed, his sword glinted in its gold scabbard and his freshly fluffed-up plumes fluttered in the breeze.

"Right, Cedric," he said. "Hop on the cart and we'll be off."

I climbed on to the mule cart next to Patchcoat.

KNIGHTMARE

As we rode out from Castle Bombast, the local villagers all ran out to wave us off.

"Hooray for Sir Percy!"

"Sir Percy for ever!"

"'E's so 'andsome!"

"And brave!"

KNIGHTMARE

Sir Percy smiled graciously and waved at his admirers.

It was remarkable. He'd completely changed his tune about the joust. He even seemed to be looking forward to it. He was much more like the hero I'd read about in *The Song of Percy*.

KNIGHTMARE

After an hour or so we came to a fork in the road. There was a signpost that pointed left to Goldentowers and right to Grimwood. To my surprise, Sir Percy took the road to Grimwood.

"But Sir Percy," I said. "The king's castle is the other way!"

"Ah, yes, dear boy," he said. "I thought we'd take the – um – scenic route."

"But won't we have to go through Grimwood?" I shuddered. Grimwood is full of bears, wolves, robbers and other nasties. The forest stretches for miles and miles and there's only one road through it. Anyone in their right mind avoids it like the plague. (There's plague in Grimwood, too.)

KNIGHTMARE

"Oh no," said Sir Percy cheerily. "We won't be going as far as that. We're just making a small detour."

The sun was setting as we rattled and jolted our way down a gloomy valley between two rocky hills.

"Ouch!" I said as the mule cart bounced out of another muddy pothole. "At this rate I don't think my bottom will survive the trip!"

On one of the hills, towering over a scruffy village, was a huge fortress. It was built of dark stone and looked black and grim against the darkening sky. Somewhere not far away a wolf started to howl.

"We'll be stopping in that village for the night," said Sir Percy.

KNIGHTMARE

"Yikes," I said. "I hope we reach it before those wolves reach us!"

It was twilight as we rolled up to the village inn. "Oi!" came a shriek from inside. "Get yer blinkin' claws out of me stew!"

A door opened and a scrawny cat shot out, followed by a woman with a filthy face and an even filthier apron.

KNIGHTMARE

"And *stay* out, you greedy fleabag!"
cried the woman. "If you want a rat to
eat, you can blinkin' well catch yer *own*!"
She hurled a wooden spoon at the cat but
it missed by a mile and bounced off
Sir Percy's helmet with a CLANG!

"My good woman, do be careful," said
Sir Percy sternly. "You might damage my
plumes."

"'Ave mercy, Yer Knightliness, 'ave
mercy!" the woman gasped, throwing
herself to her knees and grabbing
Sir Percy's foot. "Please don't fling me
in them dungeons. Anything but that!"

"*Dungeons*, dear lady? Don't be silly,"
said Sir Percy. "It was an accident. If you

can find me a room for the night I'll say no more about it."

"A room? Of course, Yer Knightliness," said the woman in delight, letting go of Sir Percy's leg. "You've come to the right place. Mistress Slopp at your service. Welcome to the Mog and Muck!"

"Excellent," said Sir Percy. "Prepare me your very best bedchamber."

"Certainly, yer honour," said Mistress Slopp. "You can have the deluxe. Sheets was cleaned last month. And you even get yer own chamber pot."

"Splendid," said Sir Percy, dismounting. "Cedric, come and see me after you've dealt with Prancelot and the trunks."

"Stables is round the back," said Mistress Slopp.

"Thanks," I said. "And where will *we* be sleeping?"

"Like I said," snapped Mistress Slopp. "Stables is round the back."

"I'm sure you'll be most comfortable, Cedric," said Sir Percy. "Now what's for dinner, dear lady? I'm starving."

"Meat stoo," said Mistress Slopp.

"What kind of meat?" asked Sir Percy.

"Er – fresh and local, yer honour," said Mistress Slopp. "Caught this very afternoon. Only the best for our guests. 'Ere, don't I recognize you? Your face looks familiar. Is you famous?"

67

But to my surprise Sir Percy said,
"Famous? Oh no, no, no. You must be
mistaken, my good woman. My name is –
er – Sir Norman de Normal."

Eh? What was all that about?

"Never 'eard of you," said Mistress
Slopp, disappointed.

Patchcoat and I went round to the stables.
We unhitched the cart and tied up
Prancelot and Gristle the mule next to an
old skinny donkey.

"Well, so much for Sir Percy's scenic
route," I said, unstrapping Prancelot's
saddle. "Why has he brought us to this

hovel? You'd think he'd prefer somewhere a bit posher."

"And what's with the false name?" asked Patchcoat. "It's not like Sir Percy to deny being famous."

"No idea," I said. "Why wouldn't he want people to know who he is?"

In one corner of the stable there was a pile of old sacks. "I suppose that'll be our bed for the night," I sighed.

"Look on the bright side," said Patchcoat. "So far I haven't seen any rats."

"True," I said. "I wonder why?"

"I dunno," said Patchcoat. "But I think I'll be giving Mistress Slopp's meat stew a miss."

Chapter Five

An Unpleasant
Peasant

By the time we'd finished sorting out
the horses it was dark. As we crossed the
yard back to the inn I nearly stepped in a
dungheap covered in flies.

"Pooh!" I said. "I reckon this qualifies as
the kingdom's *smelliest* village."

"Too right," agreed Patchcoat. "And
that castle has to be the creepiest this side

of Grimwood."

Looming above the village, the gloomy fortress looked even scarier in the last of the evening light.

"Yes," I shivered. "I wonder who lives there?"

"Don't 'ee know?" grunted the dungheap.

Patchcoat and I both leaped with fright as the dungheap rose to its feet, sending up a cloud of flies. As our eyes got used to the dim light I realized it wasn't a dungheap at all but a peasant. A shabby, ragged, filthy and *very* smelly peasant.

"That castle is the home of my boss," said the peasant, his single tooth gleaming

71

in the dark. "'E owns this village and all the land around. And I 'ope that knight of yours has got permission to be 'ere, 'cos 'e don't like trespassers, my master don't. As an 'abit of chucking 'em in his dungeons and forgettin' about 'em."

The hairs on the back of my neck started to tingle. I was beginning to get a funny feeling about this whole place. A funny, *nasty* feeling.

"And who exactly *is* your boss?" I asked, trying not to breathe in the peasant's foul stench.

"His name is Sir Roland the Rotten. And that," he said, pointing up at the grim castle on the hill, "is Blackstone Fort."

KNIGHTMARE

I left Patchcoat in the alehouse part of the inn, telling jokes to two old peasants and a dog, and dashed upstairs to Sir Percy's room. He was sitting up in bed in his undershirt.

"Sir Percy," I said. "We're right next to Blackstone Fort!"

"Correct!" said Sir Percy. "Everywhere around here belongs to Sir Roland."

"You mean – you *knew*, Sir Percy?" I gasped.

"Of course I knew," he laughed. "It's the very reason we've come to this horrible place."

KNIGHTMARE

"But why?" I asked. "If Sir Roland finds out you're here he could fling you into his dungeon and throw away the key!" *And me and Patchcoat with you*, I thought. But I kept that to myself.

Sir Percy seemed to find this terribly amusing. "But Cedric, he's not going to find out," he chuckled. "For one thing, I've cunningly used a false name." (Well, that explained that one.) "And for another, we'll be leaving here well before dawn. And when we do, we'll have made sure Sir Roland won't be taking part in the tournament."

"Really, Sir Percy?" I said. "But how?"

"Simple," said Sir Percy, though

something told me it probably wouldn't
be. "We're going to kidnap his mascot."

"His mascot? You mean Bubo the rat?"
I said.

"Precisely!" grinned Sir Percy. "You
gave me the idea yourself."

"I did?"

"Yes, dear boy! When you went on
about Sir Roland *smelling* a rat," said
Sir Percy. "If Sir Roland doesn't have his
rat, he will refuse to fight. Then, under the
rules of the joust, I will automatically be
declared the winner. Without so much as
lifting a lance. It's a foolproof plan!"

Sir Percy gave a great gleeful guffaw
and slapped his knee.

KNIGHTMARE

"But Sir Percy, that's cheating!"
I blurted. "It's totally forbidden by the
Knight's Code!"

Sir Percy's smile froze. "Now look here,
Cedric," he said sharply. "The Knight's
Code is one thing. But you, dear boy,
are bound by the *Squire's* Code. And the
Squire's Code totally forbids you to be
impudent to your master – meaning *me*."

KNIGHTMARE

"Sorry, Sir Percy," I said sheepishly. "I didn't mean to be rude. It just seems, well, wrong. And what if Sir Roland catches you?"

"Oh, there's no chance of Sir Roland catching me," said Sir Percy. "Because I'm not the one who'll be sneaking into Blackstone Fort. That, dear boy, is *your* job."

"Me?" I gasped. "But … but…"

"No buts about it," said Sir Percy. "Squire's Code, remember – you must obey your master at all times. All you have to do is enter the fort, grab the rat and bring it back. Much easier for a small, inconspicuous boy to sneak in than for a tall, good-looking and easily recognizable celebrity, such as *moi*. Think of it as a valuable knighting exercise. It'll be excellent practice for entering an enemy castle under siege."

I stood there opening and closing my mouth like a fish.

"Now, be a good chap and close the door on your way out." Sir Percy yawned. "If we're leaving before dawn I'd better grab a bit of beauty sleep."

When I got back downstairs, the dog and one of the old peasants were snoring loudly. The other was nodding off to sleep.

"I've just got time for one more joke," said Patchcoat. "Who invented King Arthur's Round Table? Sir Cumference!"

KNIGHTMARE

The other old peasant shut his eyes and started to snore.

"You've been a great audience," said Patchcoat. "Thank you and goodnight!"

While Patchcoat packed up his jester's bag, I told him what Sir Percy had asked me to do.

"The cheating chiseller!" Patchcoat said. "He should do his own dirty work!"

"I know," I said. "But maybe he's right. It *might* be easy for me to slip in unnoticed."

"Don't be daft," said Patchcoat. "You saw the fort. It's surrounded by sheer cliffs. There's only one way in and that's across the drawbridge and through the front gate. There are bound to be guards.

You've as much chance of slipping in unnoticed as an elephant with bells on."

"Maybe there's another way in," I said. "A secret passage or something…"

"Secret passage?" chuckled Patchcoat. "I think you've been reading too many fairy tales, Ced."

"No, seriously," I protested. "There's a bit in *The Song of Percy* where Sir Percy finds a secret passage into an enemy castle and single-handedly defeats a whole army."

"Just like I said, you've been reading too many fairy tales," said Patchcoat. "But look, if there *is* another way into Blackstone Fort, there is someone who might know. That smelly peasant who works for Sir Roland."

"Good idea!" I said. "But how will we find him?"

"Easy, just follow our noses!"

We found the smelly peasant snoozing in the yard under a window. I tapped him on the shoulder.

"Urrngh? Whassup?" he grunted. "It weren't me, Sir Roland, honest!"

"It's not Sir Roland," I smiled. "We met earlier, remember?"

The peasant blinked and peered at us by the dim light from the window. "Oh aye," he grunted. "You's them as didn't know about Blackstone Fort."

"Unlike your good self," said Patchcoat. "You said you worked there?"

KNIGHTMARE

"Aye. Well, I works at the fort, but not *in* the fort," said the peasant. "I works in a bit of the fort that's on the *outside* of the fort."

"This bit where you work – can you get into the rest of the fort from there?"

The peasant scratched his chin. "I s'pose so," he said. "You *could* work your way up from the bottom to the top. Or from the bottom to the *bottom*, if you're unlucky. Hur-hur-hur!" He cackled so violently that several flies flew up into the air.

I didn't have a clue what he was on about. I looked at Patchcoat and he gave me a shrug.

"So if I wanted to get into the fort that way, could you let me in?" I persisted.

KNIGHTMARE

"Well now, p'raps I could," said the peasant. "That depends, don't it?"

"Depends on what?" I asked.

But Patchcoat knew what he meant. He took a silver fourpenny piece out of his pouch. "Perhaps if I were to give you this?" he said, showing the coin.

The peasant fixed Patchcoat with a hard, beady stare. "Tuppence!" he said.

"A penny!" said Patchcoat.

"Ha'penny!" said the peasant. "And that's me final offer."

"Very well," sighed Patchcoat. "It's a deal. You drive a hard bargain, Mister…"

"Pugh," said the filthy peasant. "Hugh Pugh. But you can call me Stinky, like everyone else."

Patchcoat handed over a halfpenny coin.

"Shake on it," said Stinky Pugh, holding out a filth-encrusted hand.

Patchcoat shook it reluctantly.

"Wish me luck, Patchcoat," I said.

"Eh?" said Patchcoat. "No way am I missing out on a bit of fun in Sir Roland's castle. I'm coming with you!"

"Right, gentlemen," said Stinky Pugh. "Ready when you are. Foller me."

Chapter Six

The Tower
of Stink

The moon was hidden behind some clouds
and obviously we couldn't take torches, so
we set off from the inn in pitch-darkness.
But as we headed uphill, Patchcoat and
I had no trouble following Stinky Pugh.
As long as the stench was in front of us, we
knew we were going the right way.

To avoid bumping into a patrol of

KNIGHTMARE

Sir Roland's guards, Stinky Pugh led us on
a path well away from the main road to
Blackstone Fort. It was rough and steep, but
eventually we turned a corner and there was
the fort itself, huge and menacing against
the night sky. All that stood between us and
the main gates was a wooden drawbridge.
There was no moat, because Blackstone Fort
didn't need one. It was surrounded on all
sides by a sheer drop to the valley far below.

I seriously thought about turning
round and heading straight back to the
inn. It would serve Sir Percy right if he
had to go through with the joust. But then
again, if I disobeyed him I'd be breaking
the Squire's Code. And if he lost the joust

87

KNIGHTMARE

(I was beginning to suspect that those magic underpants might not be so magic after all), I'd probably lose my job. If that happened, who would take on a disobedient squire? I'd never get to be a knight!

We tiptoed over the drawbridge. At the end we saw a light coming from a window by the great wooden doors of the fort.

KNIGHTMARE

"That's the guardroom," whispered Stinky Pugh. "Make a sound and we're done for."

Just before the gates he led us down some steps on to a narrow ledge that ran round the base of the castle walls.

We were as quiet as mice as we ducked past the guardroom window. From inside came the sound of iron being sharpened on stone.

"Give it some elbow grease, lad!" said a voice. "That sword wouldn't slice a cucumber in 'alf, never mind an intruder!"

"Yes, Sarge," said another voice.

We hurried on and followed the ledge round the fort. I stuck close to the wall

and tried not to think about the sheer
drop below.

After a while Patchcoat whispered,
"Is it just me, or is Stinky Pugh getting
even stinkier?"

It was true. We were now round the
back of the fort, and the stench was
getting stronger and stronger. A few steps
more and the ledge stopped at a narrow
tower that jutted out of the wall. The stink
was almost overpowering. It seemed to be
coming from somewhere very close by.

"Here we are, gentlemen," grinned
Stinky Pugh. It was then that we noticed
a small door in the base of the tower. "The
back way in. What yer might call the

back passage. Hur-hur!"

"Thank goodness," I said. "The sooner we're inside, the sooner we can escape this terrible smell."

I spoke too soon.

Stinky Pugh heaved the door open and the stench that hit us was so bad it nearly knocked us over.

"Phwoargghhh!"

I can safely say it was the most EVIL smell in the world. Even thinking about it makes my nose want to jump off my face and hide.

"Welcome to my place of work, gentlemen," said Stinky Pugh. "Or should I say – welcome to the gents, gents. Hur-hur!"

KNIGHTMARE

"What?" I gasped, trying not to breathe. "You actually work – in there?"

"Aye," said Stinky Pugh proudly. "It's called a Sanitary Tower. It's the latest posh thing. Not like yer normal old-fashioned garderobe, where you sit with yer rear end dangling over the outside world in all weathers. In one o' them you does yer business and you never know where it's going to end up. 'Specially if it's a bit windy. And you get a chilly bum into the bargain. Now here" – he nodded at the tower – "it's all self-contained, see. Everything drops to the bottom of the tower. No chance of it blowing in through a downstairs window."

CALLED TO THE CHAMBER FOR AN URGENT SITTING?

Oh, where does it drop
When you go for a plop?
On the ground? In the moat?
On a guard? On a goat?
Does it land with a splat
On a fair maiden's hat?

Bid Farewell to Flying Poo Hullaballoo!
When you swap your OLD garderobe for one
of Master Norbert of Nottingham's

SANITARY TOWERS

KNIGHTMARE

"So what's your job, then?" I asked.

"I'm the Nightman," said Stinky Pugh. "One night a month I comes along with me spade and empties out the tower."

"What a terrible life of human waste," said Patchcoat.

Stinky Pugh pointed to a lit window at the top of the tower.

"See up there? That's the garderobe. It's got two doors. One leads into a corridor and the other into Sir Roland's bedchamber. It's what them posh folks calls an *en suite*. So when you gets to the top, make sure you takes the door into the corridor."

"Is it the left door or the right?" I asked, then suddenly realized what Stinky Pugh had said. "Hold on – what do you mean, when we get to the top?"

"When you gets to the top of the tower, of course," grinned Stinky Pugh. "Lucky for you I emptied it only last week."

"You mean we have to go – in there?"

"Aye," said Stinky Pugh. "It's the only way into the fort. Unless you wants to go back to the gate and ask the guards nicely? Hur-hur!"

"Looks like we haven't any choice, Ced," sighed Patchcoat.

"But how do we get up there?" I said. "Is there a ladder?"

"Nope," said Stinky Pugh. "You'll 'ave to climb."

KNIGHTMARE

"Don't worry, Ced, I've got these," said Patchcoat. He rummaged in his jester's bag and pulled out two clothes pegs.

"But how do we get out at the top?" I asked. "Isn't there a loo seat in the way?"

"The seat's only a plank with an 'ole in it," said Stinky Pugh. "You can just push the whole thing to one side."

"All right," I sighed, putting the peg on my nose. "Let's do it."

"You go first, Ced," said Patchcoat. "That way I can catch you if you fall."

"But what if you miss?" I said.

"No problem," he chuckled. "There's a soft landing at the bottom."

"Cheers, Patchcoat," I said.

96

As it turned out the tower was narrow enough to climb up by bracing our hands and feet against the sides, and it was fairly easy to get a grip on the rough stone. The inside was faintly lit by candlelight shining through the loo seat at the top. As we climbed higher and higher, and the circle of light grew bigger and bigger I began to feel a surge of excitement.

"Almost there!" I panted. "I can't believe we've nearly done it!"

KNIGHTMARE

"Shh!" said Patchcoat suddenly. "Listen!"

There was a noise above us. Someone had just opened one of the doors into the garderobe!

We stopped dead.

"Suffering siege engines!" boomed a voice. "Walter!"

I was so startled I nearly lost my grip. It was Sir Roland! Had he heard us? I held my breath as I heard Walter Warthog's familiar whine.

"You called, Sir Roland?" said Walter.

"There's no blasted hay in here," boomed Sir Roland. "Fetch some at once! Hurry!"

"Yes, Sir Roland," smarmed Walter.

KNIGHTMARE

"Of course, Sir Roland."

We heard Walter running off and returning a short time later. "Your hay, Sir Roland," he said.

"About time, too," barked Sir Roland. "The next time I come in here and there's no hay I'll use one of your stockings. Is that clear? Now get out!"

I heard Walter shuffle out of the garderobe, closing the door behind him. There was a rustle of clothing and then, without warning, the circle of light above us vanished. We were plunged into pitch-darkness.

"Uh-oh," I whispered. "I hope this doesn't mean what I think it means…"

There was a strange grunting noise, like Sir Roland was trying to lift a very heavy weight. After a few seconds the grunting stopped.

"Watch out!" hissed Patchcoat. "Backs to the wall!"

I pressed my back as flat as I could against the

wall of the tower. And not a moment too
soon.

Something whizzed past my face so
close that it knocked the peg off my nose.
A couple of seconds later there was a faint
PLOP at the bottom of the tower.

Ewww.

"That was close!" I whispered.

But Sir Roland wasn't quite done yet.
There was a funny scraping sound and
before I realized what it was, a scrunched-
up ball of hay bounced off my head and
plummeted into the smelly depths below.

The circle of light suddenly reappeared.
There was another rustle of clothing, and
the sound of the door opening and closing.

KNIGHTMARE

As soon as the coast was clear, Patchcoat burst out laughing.

"Well, Ced," he giggled. "I hope you don't get hay fever!"

"Ha-ha," I groaned. "Come on, let's get out before Sir Roland hears us."

We inched our way to the top of the tower. Like Stinky Pugh had said, it was easy enough to shove the loo seat out of the way and climb out. The worst bit was trying to do it quietly.

That and the fact it was still warm from Sir Roland's bottom.

Chapter Seven

Walter
Smells a Rat

"I've just realized something," I said, as Patchcoat climbed out after me and put back the loo seat. "We don't actually know where Sir Roland keeps his rat!"

"That's not even our first problem," muttered Patchcoat. "Stinky Pugh never did tell us which of these doors was the right one."

KNIGHTMARE

My heart sank. If we opened the wrong door we'd be face to face with Sir Roland!

It was Sir Roland himself who helped us out. "Walter!" he boomed from behind the left-hand door.

"You called, Sir Roland?"

"Fetch me some warm milk and honey from the kitchens," growled Sir Roland. "My tummy's playing up. It must be the excitement at the thought of beating that idiot Sir Percy tomorrow!"

"Of course, Sir Roland," said Walter.

"And while you're at it, nip into the Great Hall and give Bubo a bit of cheese," said Sir Roland. "The plumper he is, the more luck he brings!"

And that answered the other question.
But where was the Great Hall?

"Very good, Sir Roland," said Walter.
"At once, Sir Roland."

A few seconds later we heard Walter
hurrying past the garderobe, muttering
something about stupid rats.

"Quick," said Patchcoat. "Let's follow
him!"

"But why?" I said. "He's going to the
kitchens."

"I know," said Patchcoat. "And the
kitchens are *always* next to the Great Hall,
right? With a bit of luck we can nip into
the hall and grab the rat while Walter's
busy heating up Sir Roland's milk."

KNIGHTMARE

We slipped quietly out of the garderobe
and into the dark corridor. The only
light came from Walter's candle, some
way ahead. Keeping to the shadows, we
followed him down a long corridor lined
with the heads of stags, boars, wolves
and other startled-looking creatures
unfortunate enough to bump into Sir
Roland when he was out hunting.

KNIGHTMARE

I ducked under the outstretched claws of a whole stuffed bear – only for Patchcoat to grab me by the collar and stop me in my tracks. I soon realized why. Walter had suddenly halted just ahead of us. If I'd carried on I'd have walked straight into him!

"Pooh," Walter grumbled, sniffing the air. "What's that awful smell?"

KNIGHTMARE

Eeek! I guess after our climb up the tower, Patchcoat and I didn't exactly smell like roses. I just hoped Walter wouldn't try to find out where the stink was coming from.

"Probably Sir Roland's new hunting dogs," he muttered, as he turned a corner. "Filthy mutts. And no prizes for guessing who'll have to clear up after them."

After a few more passages and winding stairways, we reached a wide landing. The moon had come out now and it shone through the high windows on to a pair of huge wooden doors decorated with Sir Roland's coat of arms.

"The Great Hall!" whispered Patchcoat.

KNIGHTMARE

We hung back as Walter passed the hall and disappeared down a narrow flight of steps in a corner of the landing.

"That'll be the way to the kitchens," said Patchcoat. "Come on. We haven't got long!"

The door to the Great Hall opened with a loud creak. I crept inside – and jumped with fright to see a dozen knights staring back at me!

It took a moment to realize that the hall was lined with empty suits of black armour, gleaming in the moonlight. And that wasn't all. I stared in amazement at the racks of shields, swords, spears, lances, bows, arrows and other fearsome weapons.

KNIGHTMARE

"Yikes," said Patchcoat. "That's one way to impress your dinner guests! One look at this lot would put you right off your roast boar."

"Too right," I shuddered. "He's got enough weapons for a whole army!"

A long wide table ran down the entire length of the Great Hall. In the middle stood several large travelling chests, packed with weapons and armour.

"Well, well, well, what have we here?" chuckled Patchcoat. "Looks like Walter's been doing a bit of packing for the tournament." He opened his jester's bag. "Right, Ced, you grab the rat while I have a quick peek inside Sir Roland's trunks!"

KNIGHTMARE

Peering round the hall I spotted a large gilded cage tucked between suits of chainmail and some particularly vicious-looking battleaxes.

I tapped the cage and a pointy, whiskered nose poked out of a nest of straw.

"Hello, Bubo!" I said.

I carefully opened the cage and reached in to pick him up. The rat eyed me suspiciously, bared its sharp yellow teeth and then went straight for my finger.

I quickly whipped my hand out of the cage. "Vicious little so and so," I muttered.

KNIGHTMARE

"Try one of these," said Patchcoat.

He chucked a gauntlet from a suit of armour over to me. I pulled it on and this time made a grab for Bubo. He squirmed and bit at the metal glove, but I managed to lift him out and slip him into a large leather pouch I'd brought with me.

"Got you!" I said. "Come on, Patchcoat, let's get out of here!"

"Hold on, I'm almost done," he said. "A dab here, a blob there… Right, that should do it!"

"What exactly are you up to?" I said.

"Oh, I'm just preparing a couple of teensy *surprises* for Sir Roland," he grinned, holding up a pot of glue.

KNIGHTMARE

He stuffed the pot back in his jester's bag and slung it over his shoulder – just as we heard footsteps heading straight for the Great Hall!

Patchcoat whipped off his jester's cap and grabbed a pair of rusty old helmets. "It's Walter!" he said. "Quick, put this on!"

Walter stopped outside the door. "That's funny," he muttered. "I'm sure this was closed ten minutes ago." He entered the hall and sniffed. "*And* there's that nasty smell again. Bloomin' dogs. Now where's that lump of cheese?"

Walter crossed the room to Bubo's cage. Luckily he didn't notice two figures in rusty old helmets standing as still as

KNIGHTMARE

statues among the suits of armour. Bubo
was wriggling like crazy in the leather bag.
I was terrified he would start squeaking and
give us away. As soon as Walter's back was
turned, Patchcoat gave me a nudge and,
still wearing our helmets, we slunk swiftly
and silently out on to the landing.

"Which way back to the tower?" I
whispered.

"No idea," said Patchcoat.

Just then, Walter screeched. "Aargh!
The rat! The rat! Someone's stolen the rat!"

There was no time to think.

"The kitchen stairs!" I hissed. Without
saying another word we hurtled down the
stairs.

KNIGHTMARE

Just like those at Castle Bombast, the kitchens of Blackstone Fort overlooked the main courtyard. We slipped out of the kitchen door and lurked in the shadows behind a pile of empty barrels opposite the main gates of the fort.

"Now where?" I panted. "The only way out is through the main gates. But there's no chance of getting past the guards."

Suddenly, Walter burst out of the fort. He stopped dead and stared straight at us. My heart sank and my legs turned to jelly. We were done for.

KNIGHTMARE

"You there!" he cried. "There's an intruder in the fort! Search everywhere. I'll call out the rest of the watch!"

I was too stunned to reply.

"It's our helmets!" hissed Patchcoat. "He thinks we're guards!"

"Well, don't just stand there, you layabouts!" barked Walter, striding across to the guardroom. "Get a move on!"

"Yessir!" said Patchcoat. "Right away, sir!"

KNIGHTMARE

Walter banged on the door of the guardroom. "Open up! Open up!" he hollered.

"Ced," whispered Patchcoat. "I've had an idea. Stay here and try to keep out of sight."

Without another word, Patchcoat darted across the courtyard and up some steps leading to the battlements.

I quickly climbed into one of the barrels and was just wondering what on earth he was up to when Walter hurried from the guardroom. He was followed by the sergeant and half a dozen guards with swords and helmets just like the ones Patchcoat and I were wearing.

KNIGHTMARE

"Search the courtyard!" yelled Walter.
"Check inside the fort! The intruders must
still be here somewhere. They can't have
got past the gates!"

"Yes, sir!" replied the sergeant.

I ducked out of sight inside the barrel
as guards started to run all over the
courtyard. Bubo started to squeak and
I hoped with all my might that nobody
would hear him in the kerfuffle.

I was just starting to feel safe when, to
my horror, Walter spoke again.

"Sergeant," he said. "I'm going to check
in those barrels."

I heard him cross the courtyard and
start searching the empty barrels one by

one, muttering to himself as he went.

"This can't be happening," Walter said. "If Sir Roland refuses to fight that twerp Sir Percy it'll be *so* humiliating. The sooner I catch the intruder and get that stupid rat back in its cage the better."

He was two or three barrels away from me at the most. Bubo had gone quiet again but the game was definitely up. There was no escape. It was only a matter of seconds before Walter spotted me. And where was Patchcoat?

At that very instant someone cried, "I can see them, Sarge! I can see the intruders! They're escaping!"

KNIGHTMARE

The commotion in the courtyard stopped abruptly. The voice was coming from the battlements.

"Where?" called the sergeant urgently. "Where are they?"

"They've just turned off the main road to the village," came the reply. "They're heading into the next valley!"

There was something familiar about that voice from the battlements. I dared a quick peek from the barrel and in the darkness I could just make out a figure in a helmet. From where I was crouching he looked for all the world like one of the guards. But it wasn't.

It was Patchcoat!

"Open the gates!" hollered Walter, making me jump. "After them. Hurry!"

"Yes, Master Walter," said the sergeant. "All guards form pairs!"

KNIGHTMARE

The courtyard was soon alive with commotion again as guards hurried to the gates from all over the fort. Then I spotted someone trotting down the steps from the battlements and deftly weaving his way towards me through the crowd of soldiers.

"How did I do, Ced?" grinned Patchcoat. "Reckon I should join that acting troupe?"

"You were brilliant," I said. "But I still don't see how we're going to get out of here."

"Don't worry," said Patchcoat. "When I give the signal just follow me."

The guards were steadily forming two lines before the open gates.

"Swords at the ready!" ordered the sergeant. "Quick march!"

123

KNIGHTMARE

The lines started to move out of
the gate. As the pair of guards at the
back were about to move off, Patchcoat
whispered, "Got the rat?"

"Yes."

"Come on then. Quick!"

He grabbed my sleeve and swiftly
pulled me out of the shadows while the
sergeant's back was turned. A few seconds

KNIGHTMARE

later we were marching along behind the
last pair of guards.

As we crossed the courtyard I was a
bundle of nerves. Although it was dark,
our only disguise was our helmets, and
I was a lot smaller than the rest of the
guards. But as we passed through the gate
I felt elated. Patchwork's crazy plan had
actually worked! Or so I thought…

"Hey, you two at the back!" cried Walter. "Where are your swords?"

Just then a window slammed open. "WALTER! Where the devil is my milk?"

Sir Roland!

"And what the blazes is going on down there? Where are those guards off to?"

"It's really n-nothing to worry about, Sir Roland," replied Walter. "It's all under control."

"It had better be!" roared Sir Roland. "Now bring me my milk RIGHT AWAY!"

By this time Patchcoat and I were across the drawbridge. We let the soldiers go on ahead, then flung off our helmets and legged it for dear life back to the inn.

Chapter Eight

Palaver
at the Palace

When we got back to the Mog and Muck there was no time to wash, never mind change out of our stinky clothes. We had to wake Sir Percy, pack up our things and get the heck out of there. Even though Patchcoat had sent the search party off in the wrong direction, sooner or later someone from the fort was bound to come to the village asking questions. And we didn't want to be around if that someone was Walter or even – eeek! – Sir Roland himself.

We headed back the way we had come and reached the turning for Goldentowers just as the first rays of sun were lighting up the sky. In spite of our frantic departure Sir Percy was in a jolly mood.

"Excellent work, Cedric!" he chirped. "Without his mascot Sir Roland probably won't even show up today. D'you know, when we get home I *might* let you have a go on Prancelot."

"Thanks, Sir Percy!" I said. I still didn't like the idea of helping Sir Percy to cheat. But I guess if it meant I'd get to do some real knight stuff, maybe it was worth it.

I turned to check on Bubo, who was now in a battered old cage that I'd spotted at the back of Mistress Slopp's stables. As I lifted a corner of the old sack that I'd thrown over the cage to keep the rat out of sight, he peered up at me and bared his yellow teeth. I hastily pushed a piece of cheese through the bars and covered up the cage.

Patchcoat and I took it in turns to snooze as the cart bumped and lurched its way along. I was in the middle of a dream about being chased by a stuffed bear with the face of Walter Warthog when Patchcoat nudged me awake.

"We're here, Ced," he grinned. "Welcome to Goldentowers!"

I rubbed my eyes and gasped. Before me stood the biggest and most awesome building I had ever seen. The royal castle of Goldentowers gleamed in the sunshine, with bright banners hanging from its honey-coloured walls, and flags fluttering from its many turrets.

Beyond the gates to the castle grounds I could see a whole city of colourful tents and pavilions. The royal guards who lined the approach to the gates were holding back a crowd of peasants and townsfolk, who cheered and surged forward every time a knight and his entourage arrived.

And then a little girl sitting on her father's shoulders suddenly pointed at us and squealed, "There 'e is, Dad! It's 'im! It's Percy!" and the crowd started to chant:

"We all love Sir Per-cy!
We all love Sir Per-cy!
We all love Sir Per-cy!
And so say all of us!"

Sir Percy waved and nodded graciously to his fans and then, with the chants and cheers ringing in our ears, we passed across a stone bridge and through the gates into the castle grounds.

A royal herald bowed before us. "Greetings, Sir Percy!" he said. "On behalf of His Majesty the King may I welcome

you to Goldentowers. Kindly allow me to
show you to your own personal pavilion."

"Splendid!" said Sir Percy, nodding to
the herald. "Lead on!"

My heart swelled with pride as the
herald blew a blast on his trumpet and
declared, "Make way! Make way for
Sir Percy Piers Peregrine de Bluster de
Bombast!"

There were more cheers and applause
as the herald led us through the brightly
coloured tents. Fine ladies curtseyed and
noblemen and other knights bowed as we
passed. In my excitement I imagined that
they were curtseying and bowing to *me*,
Sir Cedric de Thatchbottom, as I set off on

133

my noble steed to battle the enemies of the kingdom.

"Hey, Ced, why are you waving to that duchess?" grinned Patchcoat. "That's Sir Percy's job."

"Sorry!" I blushed. "I was miles away."

Sir Percy lapped it all up, cheerfully greeting his friends in between stopping to sign copies of *The Song of Percy*.

Sir Percy's joust with Sir Roland was the talk of the tournament. And not everyone thought Sir Percy was going to win, either. While he wasn't looking, I was pestered by various traders, who handed me leaflets advertising their services.

Orlick's Oinkment

Excellent for all Wounds.

CONTAINS POOP FROM ONLY THE PRIMEST PORKERS!

Lashings of Healthy Pus or Your Money Back!

ONLY ONE APPLICATION NECESSARY!

Lance in the Leg?
Axe in the Arm?

Sawbone Sam

Will Remove Your Limbs **PAINLESSLY!**

(If you're dead.)

Bonesetter Bertha

Crunch-Click
It's Fixed in a Tick!

Hacked to Bits? Fetch

Ugbert's the Undertakers

We Pick Up the Pieces
– Literally!

THEY CARRIED HIM OFF IN AN UGBERT COFFIN!

GONE? BUT NOT FORGOTTEN!

Egfrith's Effigies

Every Tomb Should Have One! I Carve Your Face in History.

KNIGHTMARE

Eventually the herald led us to our pavilion. Patchcoat helped me to unpack the cart then went off to explore.

"I saw a sign for a jesters' joke contest," he said. "May as well go for it. See ya later, Ced!"

I began to help Sir Percy into his best armour. By the time I'd done up the last of his straps and plumped up the feathers of his best plume, a crowd of admirers had gathered outside the tent. The time for the joust was fast approaching and there was still no sign of Sir Roland.

"He's terrified of me," Sir Percy declared airily to a huddle of admiring ladies in trendy pointy hats. "He clearly

KNIGHTMARE

prefers the dishonour of refusing to fight to the humiliation of being defeated!"

That was a bit rich coming from Sir Percy. But I kept that thought to myself.

"Perhaps he's read *The Song of Percy*," gushed one of the ladies. "And he knows how foolish it is to challenge such a brave and valiant knight as yourself!"

"Too kind, dear lady, too kind," beamed Sir Percy. "You may well be right. But of course that's assuming Sir Roland *can* read!"

Sir Percy laughed heartily at his own joke while the gaggle of ladies giggled helplessly.

"Unfortunately," Sir Percy went on, clearly enjoying himself, "I rather fear that Sir Roland is more interested in eating than fighting. He's definitely getting a bit podgy these days, wouldn't you say, ladies? In fact, when Sir Roland and I were squires, do you know what we used to call him? Roly Poly! Ha, ha, ha!"

He laughed so loudly that it took him

several seconds to notice that the ladies had stopped tittering.

"Um – Sir Percy?" I said, trying to catch his attention.

"Ha, ha, ha! Roly Poly! Oh really, Cedric, don't interrupt. I'm just in the middle of—"

He looked up and suddenly went very pale indeed.

"WHAT did you just call me?" growled a familiar voice. There, red in the face, out of breath and VERY cross, stood Sir Roland the Rotten, with Walter behind him.

"Um – er – greetings, Sir Roland," stammered Sir Percy. "I – we – were just – um – admiring your – er – splendid physique, weren't we, ladies?"

Sir Percy turned round, but the ladies had all vanished.

"Oh yeah?" snarled Sir Roland. "Well, then maybe they'd like to hear what we called *you* when *you* were a squire. Percy the Plon—"

"Yes, yes, yes, never mind all that, Roland old chap!" interrupted Sir Percy. "I'm – er – delighted you could make it."

"We nearly didn't," said Sir Roland. "Seems like we had intruders in the fort last night."

"Intruders?" said Sir Percy. "How – um – unfortunate."

Walter glared in my direction.

KNIGHTMARE

I blushed and looked away.

"Yeah," glowered Sir Roland. "They glued the visors shut on my best helmets. It took Walter here ages to unstick them all, didn't it?"

"Yes, Sir Roland," said Walter.

So that's what Patchcoat was up to!

"But otherwise, no harm done," said Sir Roland. "The intruders didn't take anything."

"Really?" said Sir Percy, with a surprised glance at me. "They took *nothing*? Nothing at all?"

"That's right, Sir Percy," Walter said smugly. He stepped forward and I saw that he was holding a gilded cage.

KNIGHTMARE

I gasped. Inside the cage was a black rat!

"See you at the joust, Percy," laughed Sir Roland. "You'll be a bucket of strawberry jam by the time I've finished with you! Walter, shift yourself. I want you to make sure my lance is *extra* sharp!"

KNIGHTMARE

With that, Sir Roland stomped off. Sir Percy stared after him, then staggered backwards into the pavilion and flopped on to a chair.

"Nice try, Fatbottom," hissed Walter under his breath.

"I don't know what you're talking about," I said as innocently as I could.

"Oh no?" sneered Walter. "Then perhaps you can explain *this*. I found it in the Great Hall."

He put his hand into his tunic and pulled out Patchcoat's cap. He flung it at my feet and turned to follow Sir Roland.

"And by the way, Stinkbottom," he called over his shoulder. "You *stink*!"

KNIGHTMARE

I stood and gawped at Walter's back as he strutted off, carrying the black rat with him.

"Cedric!" Sir Percy's quavering voice interrupted my thoughts. "Kindly step inside. I'd like a quick word."

Chapter Nine

Joust in Time

"Well now, dear boy," said Sir Percy. "It seems like you kidnapped the wrong rat."

"But I *did* catch the right rat, honest, Sir Percy," I said. I went into the corner of the pavilion where I had put Bubo safely out of sight, and lifted a corner of the old sack that covered the cage. "See? Walter must have found a replacement."

KNIGHTMARE

But Sir Percy didn't seem angry. To my surprise he had a big grin on his face. Maybe he was finally resigned to doing the honourable thing and actually *fighting* Sir Roland.

"Never mind, never mind. We all make mistakes," he said. "However, I am a man of my word, so I intend to keep my promise about letting you have some proper knighting experience."

"Really?" I said in delight. "Can I ride Prancelot around Castle Bombast? Just once?"

"Oh, no need to wait until we get home, dear boy," he smiled. "I am hereby giving you the honour of jousting against

KNIGHTMARE

Sir Roland at this very tournament. Just keep your visor shut and no one will know it isn't me."

So that's why he looked so happy. He had no intention of fighting at all!

"But Sir Percy," I protested. "The Knight's Code clearly states that anyone caught impersonating a knight will be banished from the kingdom!"

"And the *Squire's* Code clearly states that a squire must *never* refuse a present from his knight," said Sir Percy. "You know what they say – never look a gift horse in the mouth, eh?" He chuckled at his own joke. "Now let's get this armour off me and on to you."

KNIGHTMARE

"But Sir Percy, I've only ever ridden Gristle the mule," I pleaded, reluctantly helping him to unstrap his breastplate. "And I don't know how to fight!"

"Mule shmule," grinned Sir Percy. "A horse is just the same. Sit on its back, hold on tight and off you go. Just point your lance at Sir Roland and try to knock him off his horse. Don't worry if you miss. You get three goes."

"Three goes?" I said.

"Yes, dear boy," said Sir Percy. "Three goes with a lance, three with a sword and three with a mace. That's all there is to it. All a bit of fun really. Think of it as an excellent way to acquire some top-notch

148

knighting skills."

Eeek! An excellent way to end up *dead*, more like.

Sir Percy's armour was way too big for me. I stuffed it with several armfuls of hay, but I still rattled around in it like a pea in a dungeon.

"Right, now you'd better hurry up and get on Prancelot," said Sir Percy. "I'd be delighted to give you a hand, but I have to stay out of sight. Good luck!"

Patchcoat was still off at the joke contest so I had to mount Prancelot on my own. It was only when I tried to get into the saddle that I realized quite how enormous she was. Gristle the mule was

KNIGHTMARE

one thing, but a walloping great warhorse was something else entirely.

I put my foot in the stirrup and tried to heave myself up, but I toppled flat on my back under the weight of the armour.

Prancelot looked down at me and gave a snort.

KNIGHTMARE

I struggled to my feet, took a deep breath and muttered, "Three-two-one– HUP!" This time I hauled myself up into the saddle – and almost toppled over the other side. I'd just managed to drag myself up when a man in grand robes appeared.

"Baron Buskin Fitztightly," he said with a nod. "Chief Herald of His Majesty the King. Sir Percy, it is time for your joust with Sir Roland. Allow me to lead you to the lists."

I gave Prancelot a gentle prod with my feet and held on tight as she headed for the jousting ground. It was tricky to keep my balance *and* hold Sir Percy's lance. And to make things worse, it was starting to rain.

KNIGHTMARE

I can't believe I'm doing this, I thought.
*I can't believe I've ended up with a knight
who's such a wuss.*

Ahead of me I saw the special
tournament grandstand where all the
top lords and ladies in the kingdom were
waiting to watch the joust, sheltered from
the rain. I was shaking with nerves so
much that I was sure Sir Percy's armour
would start rattling.

My heart leaped into my mouth as
I entered the narrow track where the
joust was to take place. I saw the faces of
all the spectators turn towards me and
knew there was no way I could wriggle out
of this now.

KNIGHTMARE

And then something weird happened.

The aristocratic crowd began to
applaud and cheer. Ladies cried, "We
love you, Sir Percy!" and started throwing
me flowers and ribbons and silk scarves.
For a few amazing moments I forgot how
terrified (and stupid) I was and felt what it
was like to be a *real* knight.

But only for a few moments. All of a
sudden the crowd stopped cheering and went,
"Ooooh!" as they looked away from me
towards the other end of the jousting ground.

Entering the lists directly opposite
me was Sir Roland the Rotten. Wearing
his best blood-red armour and a bronze
boar's head on his helmet, he looked even

more terrifying than usual. In one hand
he wielded a particularly sharp-looking
lance. In the other was the black rat. It
was wriggling a lot and Sir Roland seemed
to be having a problem keeping it under
control. A handful of people in the crowd
cheered, "Go on, Sir Roland!" but most of
them remained silent.

KNIGHTMARE

Sir Roland's visor was up. Mine, of course, was firmly shut.

"Too scared to show your face, eh, Percy?" he boomed.

His few fans tittered. The rat squirmed. The rain began to bucket down. It dripped into the slits in my visor and made it harder to see.

Then several trumpets sounded a fanfare and the chief herald announced, "Pray silence for the king and queen!"

I gasped. For the first time I looked properly at the figures seated on large thrones in the centre of the grandstand. They were both wearing crowns and I realized that not only was I about to look an utter idiot – and possibly a dead idiot at that – but I was going to do it in front of none other than the king and queen. As I had this thought the king stood up and the crowd fell completely silent.

"Sir Percy and Sir Roland, I bid you welcome to the tournament," the king boomed. He was a tall man with a red face and an impressive black beard with a big white streak in it. From the way he filled out his splendid purple and green royal robes, I'd definitely say he was fond of the odd roast boar or two.

"Now then, chaps," the king went on heartily. "I like nothing more than a jolly good joust, so I'm relying on you to give me and the queen here a tip-top afternoon's entertainment, eh? Oh, if I were just a few years younger I'd be down there like a shot duelling with the pair of you. Just like at that tournament when—"

"Ahem!" said the queen in a very loud whisper. "Do get on with it, Fredbert. The guests are getting peckish."

KNIGHTMARE

"Quite right, my dear. Mustn't delay the after-joust banquet, eh?" the king guffawed. "Knights, let the joust begin!"

The crowd held its breath. The only sound was the *clunk!* of Sir Roland's visor as he slammed it shut.

He lifted his lance and pointed it straight in my direction. Then he jabbed his horse with his heels and before I knew it a massive red mountain of metal was heading my way.

Right, this is it. I thought to myself. *Why did I ever agree to this crazy plan?*

Now Sir Roland was charging at full gallop, his horse's hooves pounding the earth like thunder.

KNIGHTMARE

I was trembling so much that I lost my
balance and had to dig my heels hard into
Prancelot's side to stop myself slipping out
of the saddle.

Unfortunately, she took this as a
command to charge and moments later
we were galloping headlong in the rain
towards Sir Roland.

"Go for it, Sir Percy!" cheered the crowd.

It was all I could do to cling on for
grim life, my heavy lance swaying all
over the place as the gap between me and
Sir Roland got narrower and narrower.

Suddenly, we were almost level. I could
see Sir Roland's black rat scramble up
on to his helmet as he aimed his lance

right at my heart.

I ducked just in the nick of time!
I nearly fell off, but at least Sir Roland
had missed me.

Then I heard a metallic clunk and a
great "oooh!" from the crowd. It was only
when I heard the king declare, "One hit to
Sir Percy!" that I turned to see what had
happened. Sir Roland had removed his
helmet and was inspecting it. He looked
furious. I spotted the boar crest lying on
the ground. By some fluke, my lance must
have knocked it off!

"You'll pay for this, Percy!" fumed
Sir Roland.

"Knights, prepare for your second

pass," declared the king.

I gulped. I doubted I'd be so lucky next time.

And then I heard laughing, and someone shouted, "Look at Sir Roland!"

I glanced up to see Sir Roland with something wet and furry attached to his face.

"Gerroff!" he bellowed. "Blasted rat! Bit me on the nose! He's never done that before!"

He succeeded in detaching the rat from his nose. But where the rat had been there was now a large black stain. The spectators roared with laughter.

"He's got a black nose!"

"Look at his armour!"

"The rat's leaking!"

KNIGHTMARE

It was true. The rain was washing streaks of black dye off the rat and all over Sir Roland's polished red armour!

I gasped in astonishment. But that was nothing compared to Sir Roland's reaction. Before his very eyes, the rat was turning from black to a very normal brown.

"This isn't Bubo!' he roared. "I can't possibly fight without Bubo. Walter!"

The king stood up. "Sir Roland, will you please hurry up and begin the joust?"

"I will, Your Majesty," spluttered Roland. "Just as soon as I find my mascot. WALTER!"

"Nonsense," said the king. "I'm not hanging about in this rain while you hunt for some silly rat. I declare Sir Percy the winner!"

He then nodded at me and said, "Well done, old chap. Tonight you shall have a place of honour at the royal table. Double helpings of peacock pie for you."

And with that, the king and queen swept from the royal box.

KNIGHTMARE

The crowd cheered as I rode from the
lists. The moment I reached our pavilion
I dismounted and dived inside.

Sir Percy was delighted when I told him
what had happened.

"Splendid!" he cried. "Now hurry up
and get that armour off. I need you to help
me dress for dinner. A victorious knight
must look his best for his admirers!"

"Yes, Sir Percy," I said. "Otherwise
they might think you *hadn't* just won a
joust."

Sir Percy, I thought, *you owe me one.
Big time.*

KNIGHTMARE

Just then Patchcoat came running in. He was covered in rotten fruit and vegetables.

"Hello, Patchcoat," I said. "I'm guessing you didn't win the joke contest."

"Well, no," said Patchcoat. "But I got a great reaction from the crowd."

"So Walter must have caught a *normal* brown rat and dyed it black," said Patchcoat. "Quite clever, really."

"Yeah," I said. "If it hadn't nearly got me half killed."

We were on the way back to Castle Bombast and just approaching the

turn-off for Blackstone Fort. Patchcoat
and I sat in the mule cart behind a
beaming Sir Percy, while a royal herald
trumpeted my master's 'victory' in every
village we passed through. *Hmmph.*

"Mind you, I do feel just a teensy-weensy
bit sorry for Walter," said Patchcoat. "Sir
Roland was SO cross with him for losing
Bubo! One of the other jesters heard him
giving Walter a month's toilet-cleaning
duty. Apparently he'll be working with our
old friend Stinky Pugh."

I took Bubo out of his bag and gave him
a stroke. I was actually growing quite fond
of the little feller.

"Talking of Stinky Pugh," I said.

KNIGHTMARE

"I'm definitely having a bath as soon as we – OW!"

I yelped as the rat sank its yellow teeth into my finger, then leaped off the cart and scuttled off in the direction of Blackstone Fort. As I watched, Bubo turned and gave me one last look.

I could have sworn he was smiling.

Take a peek at the first chapter
of Cedric's next adventure:

Feast Fight!

SWISH!

"*Eeek!*"

THUNK! TWOINNNG!!!!

"Ah, I think we'll call that a warm-up
shot, Cedric," said Sir Percy, lowering his bow.
"Now be a good fellow and fetch the arrow."

"Y-yes, Sir Percy."

I picked myself up out of the mud, walked
shakily to the large oak tree and pulled out

KNIGHTMARE

Sir Percy's arrow. It was *exactly* where I'd been standing just a few seconds earlier.

"Shift the target a bit to the left," he said. "Those trees are spoiling my line of sight."

"Yes, Sir Percy," I sighed. For the zillionth time that morning I lugged the target to a new spot. Sooner or later he might actually hit it. Just as long as he didn't hit me first.

"That's better," said Sir Percy. "And don't stand so close to it. It puts me off my aim."

I *hadn't* been standing close the last time. I'd been sheltering somewhere nice and safe – or so I'd thought. If I hadn't dived out of the way, Sir Percy would have needed a new squire for the second time in three months.

A knight is supposed to teach his squire

proper knighting skills. But somehow my master – known to his many fans as Sir Percy the Proud – never quite gets round to it. Just like that morning, when he'd said he *might* let me have a go with the bow once he'd 'warmed up'. Two hours of 'warm-up shots' later, I obviously wasn't going to be firing my first arrow any time soon. I can safely say that Sir Percy couldn't hit a castle gate if it was right in front of his nose. Actually, make that a *castle*.

Could this really be the same famous knight who once shot a secret message tied to an arrow through the arrow-slit of a besieged castle? From half a mile away? At night? Blindfolded? It's one of the best bits of *The Song of Percy*, Sir Percy's wildly popular account of his knightly deeds. Hmmm. It wasn't the first time I'd wondered whether *The Song of Percy* might be a bit … exaggerated.

He notched another arrow to his bow and I quickly checked for a safe place to fling myself the moment he fired.

"Ready, Cedric?"

"Ready, Sir Percy."

All of a sudden I heard the sound of hooves among the trees. But before I could say anything, a gust of wind blew Sir Percy's dashing new green and orange velvet hunting cap over his eyes.

TWANGGG!

KNIGHTMARE

"Bother!"

Sir Percy fired blindly into the air.
I leaped for cover but luckily his arrow
flew high over the trees.

"Blasted breeze!" said Sir Percy, pushing
the cap off his eyes. "Ah well. No harm d—"

"Aargh!!"

There was a startled yell and a whinny.
Then a grandly dressed man rode out of the
trees looking alarmed – and very cross. Sir
Percy's arrow was sticking out of his saddle,
right between his legs. A couple of inches
the wrong way and … ouch!

"This is an outrage!" roared the rider,
who looked vaguely familiar. "Raining
arrows on me! I could have been cut off

in my prime!"

"My sincerest apologies," said Sir Percy. "It was the wind."

"I don't care about your personal problems," said the man. He yanked the arrow out of his saddle and flung it at Sir Percy's feet. "Next time, mind where you're shooting, you careless twerp!"

"Now, look here," scowled Sir Percy, puffing out his chest. "I will have you know that I, Sir Percy Piers Peregrine de Bluster de Bombast, will not be spoken to in that tone by the likes of-of—"

"Fitztightly," fumed the man. "Baron Buskin Fitztightly. Chief Herald of His Majesty the King."

Coming Soon!

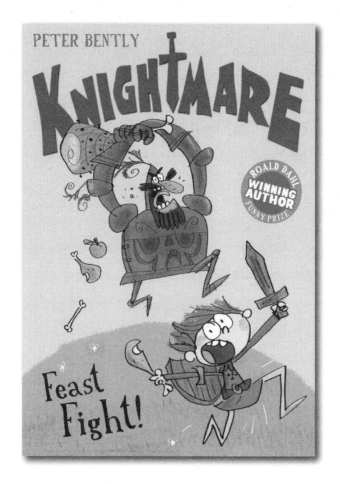